PLAYS FOR PERFORMANCE

A series designed for
contemporary production and study
Edited by
Nicholas Rudall and Bernard Sahlins

SOPHOCLES

Oedipus
the King

In a New Translation by
Nicholas Rudall

Ivan R. Dee
CHICAGO

Library of Congress Cataloging-in-Publication Data:
Sophocles.
    [Oedipus Rex. English]
    Oedipus the King / Sophocles ; in a new translation by Nicholas Rudall.
        p. cm. — (Plays for performance)
    ISBN 1-56663-307-9 (cloth : alk. paper) —
    ISBN 1-56663-308-7 (pbk. : alk. paper)
    1. Oedipus (Greek mythology)—Drama.   I. Rudall, Nicholas.   II. Title.   III. Series.
PA4414.O7 R83 2000
882'.01—dc21   00-025059

INTRODUCTION

by Nicholas Rudall

Forty years ago when I was an undergraduate at Cambridge University, I attended a series of lectures on *Oedipus the King* given by Denys Page, the Regius Professor of Greek. My best fiend and I had profound—so we thought—intellectual disagreements with the foremost classicist in the world. Given the educational structure of that time, we had no other recourse but to *write* to him and express our opinions. Despite his pronouncements, this could not be a tragedy, we said, because when the play begins Oedipus has already killed his father, married his mother, and produced four doomed children. This was *fated*, we said. There was no escape. Therefore there could be no blame, no sin, no guilt. Our handwritten letter was returned to us a few days later. We had listed the above objections and perhaps half a dozen others. Beside each objection Professor Page had written: Wrong! . . . wrong! . . . wrong! . . . *possibly* . . . wrong! and . . . just once . . . Right!

I am not sure now how I felt about such a dismissal. Except that he was right. The world of Athenian intellectuals in the fifth century was faced constantly with the paradox faced, for example, by St. Augustine and all others who accept an omnipotent God or a manifest destiny: if God or Fate decides everything, can there be free will? Of course these cross-cultural terms are anachronistic and potentially misleading.

But I believe some permutation of them is at the heart of the unbearable glory of this play.

Oedipus is a great leader. He is determined to save his city. It is his passion, his compassion, and his intellect that destroy him. It is *his free choice* to unearth the truth. The unspoken premise of Sophocles' play is that if all were left alone, untouched, unexamined, there would be no blinding, no death, and most important no understanding—not an understanding of why, but an understanding of the insignificance of mortal aspirations. The seeing man is blinded by the truth. The king is made a beggar. And his children will not escape the curse of Fate. But they will struggle and think and fight. We are left to contemplate our microscopic place in an incomprehensible universe.

The translations in this series are meant primarily for the stage. Their premise is that the words should be immediate and speakable by American actors. But they go beyond that. There have been, for example, sublime translations of Greek tragedies, whether by Gilbert Murray or Grene and Lattimore. Our admittedly precise task is to make the ancient words immediately accessible. When an "ancient Greek" listened to Euripides, he did not hear some pastiche of Victorian diction, he heard his own tongue ringing true. Our aim is to make these ancient words speak in a voice that resonates with ours.

CHARACTERS

OEDIPUS
PRIEST of Zeus
CREON, brother of the queen
TEIRESIAS, a prophet
JOCASTA, the queen
MESSENGER
SHEPHERD of Laius
SECOND MESSENGER
CHORUS of Theban elders
ANTIGONE, daughter of Oedipus
ISMENE, daughter of Oedipus
BOY

Oedipus the King

OEDIPUS: My children, you who live in the heart of this
our city, living sons of ancient Cadmus, why have
you come to these sacred altars? Why do you bring
garlands and kneel in supplication to the gods?
The city is laced with the breath of incense.
The air quivers with lamentation and with prayer.
My children, I did not want to hear your desires
    from messengers.
Therefore I have come in person to hear you
    speak—I, Oedipus your king.
(to a Priest) You there, since you are the eldest,
    speak on their behalf.
Tell me what is troubling you. Do you come in fear?
Do you seek a blessing from the gods?
Tell me. Never doubt that I will help you in every
    way I can.
I am moved and touched to find you suppliant
    here.

PRIEST: Oedipus, great king of Thebes!
You see before you clinging to the altar's steps men
    of all ages. Here are boys too young to be alone.
    Here are priests weighed down with time, priests
    of Zeus—as I am. Here are young men as yet un-
    married. And thousands more, olive wreaths in
    their hair, throng the public squares. They hud-
    dle before the two shrines of Athena and at
    Apollo's temple where the god speaks in the
    glowing embers of his fire. Your eyes see the
    truth: Thebes is drowning in a deadly sea, is sink-
    ing beneath the waves of death.

There is a blight that eats the budding fruits of the earth.

Our cattle die. Women give birth to stillborn children. A deadly plague consumes our city, strikes like bolts of lightning, burns our flesh, and ravages the house of Cadmus. My lord, we are plunged into darkness. Death alone grows fat upon our agony.

We have come to you to offer our prayers.

We know you are no god.

But of all men you are the most wise in the ways of god.

You saved us from the Sphinx, who sang her doom from the stone of her breast.

You saved us from her plague. You knew no more than we, we could not teach you.

But you saved us when a god touched your mind.

Therefore, great King of Thebes, we turn to you.

Save us. Heal us. Listen to the gods. Listen to the minds of mortals.

Your wisdom saved us long ago.

It can save us now when troubles seethe again.

You are the pinnacle of nobility, give us back our lives.

Remember that we call you the Liberator.

Remember that we love you for your courage long ago. Let not the world remember you as the king who once was great but then fell from greatness.

Save the ship of state from the storm.

Once, years ago, you turned our unhappiness to joy.

You can do it once more.

You rule this land. No man disputes your power.

But rule over the living, not the dead.

When no men throng the streets, the city walls are nothing and our proud ships mere empty shells.

OEDIPUS: Oh my poor children. I understand the passions that brought you here.

I know that you are plagued with sickness. Yet sick as you are, not one as sick as I.

What each of you suffers is your own pain, no one else's.

But I suffer for you, for my city, and for myself.

I was not asleep. You are not waking me.

I have been weeping for a long time.

I have paced my restless room thinking, thinking.

In the end I found a remedy and I have put it to work:

I have sent Creon, son of Menoeceus, brother of the queen, to Delphi. There at Apollo's oracle he will learn, if he can, what I must do or promise to do to save the city.

I have been counting the days and I am troubled. For he should have returned.

What can be keeping him? This is the day! He should be here.

But whenever he returns I will do what the god orders.

PRIEST: Your promise is given in good time. They say that Creon is here.

OEDIPUS: Oh Lord Apollo, may his news shine as bright as the hope on his face.

PRIEST: The news must be good. He is crowned with laurel, a wreath thick with berries.

OEDIPUS: We shall soon know. See where he comes.

(Creon enters)

OEDIPUS: Oh brother, Prince of Thebes, what answer do you bring us from Apollo?

CREON: A powerful answer. Our deep agonies will be healed if they are treated right.

OEDIPUS: What did the oracle say? Your words are ambiguous. I still hover between hope and fear.

CREON: Do you wish me to speak in public in front of all these men? I will of course. But should we not go inside?

OEDIPUS: Let them hear. For I suffer for them more than for myself.

CREON: Then I will tell you what I heard. In plain words, the oracle commands us to expel from Thebes an old pollution. We are sheltering a thing that is killing us and is beyond cure.
We cannot let it feed upon us any longer.

OEDIPUS: What pollution? How are we to expel it from our midst?

CREON: By exile or by death. Blood must answer for blood.
A murder blew the deadly plague breath on our city.

OEDIPUS: A murder? Whose? Did the god not name the man?

CREON: My lord, Laius once was our king before you came to rule over us.

OEDIPUS: I know. I never saw the man, but others told me of him.

CREON: He was murdered. Apollo demands that we take revenge upon the man who killed him.

OEDIPUS: Where are the killers? How, after so many years, can we find a clue to solve the crime?

CREON: Apollo said the killer is amongst us. We must search and be aware of everything.

OEDIPUS: Where was he killed? In the palace or outside the city or in some other country?

CREON: He told us that he was going to the shrine of a god. He never came home again.

OEDIPUS: Was there no witness . . . some attendant to tell what happened?

CREON: They were all killed. Except for one.
He escaped, but his terror made him forget all but one thing.

OEDIPUS: What was that? That one thing may be the key that unlocks this whole mystery.

CREON: He said a band of highwaymen attacked them. They were outnumbered and the king was killed.

OEDIPUS: Strange that highwaymen should be so bold . . . unless they were bribed by some faction from the city.

CREON: We considered that. But when Laius was killed the city was besieged with other troubles. There was no time for vengeance.

OEDIPUS: What troubles could have stopped you from finding the killer of your king?

CREON: The Sphinx. Her riddles stopped our ears and brought destruction.

OEDIPUS: Once again I must bring the darkness into the light.
Apollo is right to show, as you do, this concern for the dead.
I will obey his command. I will stand by your side. I will avenge this country's loss.

Hubris

13

It is my duty. I do it not for some unknown friend
but for myself.
We must expel this evil.
Whoever killed King Laius might be the death of
me—who knows?
It might happen even now.
It is in my own interest to avenge your slaughtered
king.
My children, leave the altar's steps. Raise the olive
branches to the sun.
Call the elders of Thebes to gather here. Tell them
I will do all that is in my power.
With the god's help we will be saved. Without it we
are lost.

PRIEST: Rise up, my children. We came to hear just
this. And our king has given his word.
Apollo has sent us an oracle.
May he walk among us and heal us and drive this
plague from our city.

(all exit)

CHORUS: Oh sweet voice of Apollo
You bring the truth of Zeus
To Thebes from your shrine of gold.
What do you say to us?
My heart trembles with fear.

Apollo, God of Healing, hear us!
Do you cast upon us a grief unknown before
Or in the circle of time awaken a remembered
doom?
Immortal voice, golden child of Hope, speak to us.

We pray to Athena. Daughter of Zeus, defend us.
We pray to Artemis of Thebes, her sister.
Come to us now, throned on high above your peo-
ple.

14

We pray to Apollo, distant archer.
Once, when we were in the jaws of death,
You drove the burning plague from us.
Come to us now, defend us.
You three powers of heaven,
Descend and save us.

Ah what griefs uncountable are ours.
Our people are sick and dying.
No man has the will to fight the god of death.
The gentle earth lies barren.
Women in labor groan in vain.

Body falls upon body
Swifter than the flight of birds
Swifter than the wave of fire
Racing to the shores of Night.

Corpses litter the city streets.
Death feeds upon death.
Infection breeds, and there is
No time to mourn the uncountable dead.

Old gray women flock to the altars,
Weep, and rend the air with prayers
And cries of grief:
Apollo, heal us!
Athena, golden child of Zeus,
Turn your shining face upon our pain. ⟶

collective prayer

The War god stalks our streets,
No sword in hand and yet we die.
Fire encircles our screams.
Send him to the Ocean's depths
Into the waves that kill the flames.
What life survives the night
Dies in tomorrow's sun.
Zeus, turn your fire upon him,
With lightning strike the god of War.

Apollo, stretch tight your golden bow,
Loose your arrows in our defense.
Artemis, race across our hills
In a blaze of saving light.
Dionysus, God of Thebes,
Come to us with your shock of golden curls,
Flushed with wine in the whirlwind
Ecstasy of your followers.
Destroy the loathsome god of Death
In the conflagration of your joy.

(enter Oedipus)

OEDIPUS: I hear your prayer. Listen to me and I will teach you how to heal.

You will find comfort and relief.

I knew nothing of this story of Laius's death, knew nothing of the deed itself.

How could I therefore solve a crime alone?

But now, since I became a citizen after the murder, I make this proclamation to all my fellow Thebans: If anyone knows the man who killed King Laius, I order him to tell me everything. He must not be afraid for his long silence. No, I promise that he will not be punished with death but may leave this land in safety. If any man knows that the killer was a foreigner, let him speak out at once.

He shall have my thanks and a rich reward. But if you remain silent and attempt to protect yourself or a friend and ignore my commands, hear what I will do:

I forbid the people of this country, where I am king, ever to harbor the killer or speak to him. Give him no place at your prayers or sacrifices. Hound him from your homes. For he it is who defiles our city. This the oracle has shown to me.

And I hereby join with the god as champion of
our murdered king.

I lay this curse upon the killer, whether he acted
alone or with accomplices:

May your life be a searing agony!

This curse I even turn upon myself. For if it turns
out that the killer breaks my bread and shares
my hearth, I too must suffer. This is my command. Obey it for my sake, for Apollo, and for
our country, which lies barren and diseased
through the anger of heaven.

Let us suppose the oracle had not spoken.

Should the murder of your king, your noble king,
go unavenged?

This pollution had to be purged clean.

And now that I sit upon that great man's throne,
possess his wife, his bed, fathering children as
would he if he had lived, I will be his avenger.
For had not fate cut him down he might have
produced a son, a brother to my children.

I now will become that son, as though in truth I
were, and I will hunt the killer down.

Vengeance for Laius, son of Labdacus, descendant
of great Cadmus and King Agenor!

If any men disobey my commands, may the gods
make their crops wither in the fields, may they
never see the fruit of their loins, may they rot on
earth. But to you who are loyal to me and ap-
prove what I have done, I pray that Justice and
all the gods look kindly upon you forever more.

CHORUS: I swear to you my lord that I accept your
commands.

I did not kill the king nor do I know who did.

My advice is this . . . Apollo posed the question . . .
he should give the answer and tell us who the
murderer is.

OEDIPUS: Your advice is well taken. But no man can force the gods to speak against their will.

CHORUS: May I then suggest a second plan?

OEDIPUS: And a third if need be.

CHORUS: My lord, if any man can speak with the god it is Teiresias. He might bring us to the light.

OEDIPUS: I have already done it. Creon suggested it. And I have sent for him. I am surprised he is not here.

CHORUS: My mind is stirring now. Rumors from long ago. Mere gossip.

OEDIPUS: Tell me. I want to know everything.

CHORUS: It was said that he was killed by travelers.

OEDIPUS: That is what I heard. But no one knows the man who saw him die.

CHORUS: Well, if he knows what fear is, he will run in terror of your curse.

OEDIPUS: A man who can do a thing like that is not afraid of words.

CHORUS: But here comes one who can capture him.
Here is Teiresias, whose mind is fired by the god and in whom truth lives and breathes.

(enter Teiresias, led by a boy)

OEDIPUS: Teiresias, our prophet, you understand all things—the hidden mysteries of the wise, the high things of heaven, and the low things of the earth.
Though your eyes cannot see, you know of this plague that infects our city.
We turn to you—our one defense—our shield.

18

No doubt the messengers told you what Apollo
said in his reply to us:
One course alone can free us from this plague . . .
we must find the murderers of King Laius.
We must execute them or expel them from this
land.
Therefore give us freely of your gift of prophecy.
Save yourself, your country, and your king.
Save all the people from this pollution of spilled
blood. We are in your hands.
There is no greater honor than for a man to serve
his fellow men.

TEIRESIAS: Alas! It is a miserable thing to be wise when
wisdom brings no reward. I had forgotten that ancient truth. Otherwise I would not be here.

OEDIPUS: What is wrong? Why this melancholy mood?

TEIRESIAS: Let me go home. Do not keep me here. It
would be best if you bear your burden and I mine.

OEDIPUS: For shame!
No true-born Theban would withhold his gift of
prophecy from the country that he loves.

TEIRESIAS: Your words, my king, lie far from the truth.
I am afraid that I, like you, will not speak true.

OEDIPUS: Oh speak! Hold nothing back. I order you to
tell us what you know.
We are your suppliants.

TEIRESIAS: Yes . . . but you do not know what you are
asking me.
I will never reveal my miseries . . . or yours.

OEDIPUS: What!! You know something but will not
speak?
Will you betray us and destroy the state?

TEIRESIAS: I will not hurt myself or you. Why ask from me what I will never tell?

OEDIPUS: You are a wicked man. Your silence would anger a lifeless stone.
Will nothing loosen your tongue, melt your heart, shake you out of this implacable silence?

TEIRESIAS: You blame me but you do not see yourself. In your anger you turn on me.

OEDIPUS: Who could be calm when he heard you scorn the desperation of our city?

TEIRESIAS: Well, whether I speak or not, what will be will be.

OEDIPUS: That is true. And your duty is to tell me.

TEIRESIAS: I have nothing more to say. You can rage to your heart's content.

OEDIPUS: Yes, I am angry and *I* will not be silent! I will speak what is on my mind.
I think it was you, yes you, who planned the murder.
Yes—and did it all—except the actual killing.
And if you were not blind you would have done that too.

TEIRESIAS: Is that so? Then hear me! I call upon you to obey the words of your own decree.
From this day on do not speak to me or to these citizens.
You are the killer. *You* bring the pollution upon Thebes.

OEDIPUS: Hold your slanderous tongue.
You taunt me and think because you are a prophet you will go scot-free.

TEIRESIAS: I *am* free. For my strength lies in the truth.

OEDIPUS: Who made you say this? You didn't find this accusation through your art.

TEIRESIAS: You made me speak. You provoked me against my will.

OEDIPUS: I made you speak?? Then speak again. Make clear your charges.

TEIRESIAS: Did you not understand the first time? Will you provoke me yet again?

OEDIPUS: I half understood your meaning. Speak again.

TEIRESIAS: I say you are the murderer of the man whose murderer you seek.

OEDIPUS: You will regret repeating so foul a slander.

TEIRESIAS: Must I go on and inflame your anger even more?

OEDIPUS: You can say all you want. It will be a waste of breath.

TEIRESIAS: I say that you are living in darkest shame with the closest of your family.
And you know nothing of your sin.

OEDIPUS: Do you think that you can keep on spewing out your filth and get away with it?

TEIRESIAS: Yes, if there is strength in truth and truth does not die.

OEDIPUS: Truth lives in other men but not in you.
For you, in ear, in mind, in eye, in everything are blind.

TEIRESIAS: Poor fool! You lay words upon me which soon all men will lay upon you.

OEDIPUS: You are a child of endless darkness, and you have no power over me or any man who can see the light of the sun.

TEIRESIAS: True, I have no such power over you. Your fate is in the hands of Apollo.

OEDIPUS: Is this plot yours alone or was it Creon's idea?

TEIRESIAS: Not Creon. You bring destruction upon yourself.

OEDIPUS: Wealth! Power! The art of being a ruler!
Kingship! The admiration of one's subjects!
What envy these things breed—if Creon, Creon whom I trusted, who was my friend, seeks in secret to overthrow me.
All for this position of majesty which the city gave to me though I did not seek it.
He has bought the services of this charlatan, this fraud, this scheming beggar-priest.
With *money* in his hands his eyes can see. But his art is stone blind.
You there! Tell me! When did you ever prove that you were a true prophet? When the Sphinx was destroying the city with her riddles, why could you not save these people?
The riddle could not be solved by guessing.
It needed the true art of prophecy. And you were found wanting.
Neither the birds of the air nor the configurations of the stars could help you.
It was I, I who came here, Oedipus, an ordinary simple man.
I stopped the mouth of the Sphinx. I did not need omens.

I needed only my native wit. And you seek to overthrow me?

You hope to reign with Creon in my place?

You will regret it, you and your friend Creon.

If it weren't for your age you would feel the pain
that your treachery deserves.

CHORUS: You both are angry. But now is not the time
for fury.

We must decide how we can best obey the oracle.

TEIRESIAS: You are the king. But I have the right to
speak my mind freely.

In this I too am a king. I have no master but Apollo.
I am his servant.

You cannot accuse me of being allied with Creon.

This is my answer: since you mocked my blindness,
know that though you have eyes you cannot see
how low you have fallen.

You do not know in whose house you live, no, nor
with whom.

Who is your father, who is your mother? You do not
know.

In ignorance you live as an enemy to the living and
the dead.

But the curse of your parents one day will drive you
wounded from this land.

Those eyes that now see clear day will be covered
with darkest night.

Your cries will echo on every hill. Cithaeron will
ring with your moans. For you will know that the
marriage hymns that welcomed you to Thebes
were a dirge of mourning for your ill-fated re-
turn.

All this will come to pass—and more—before you
find your children and yourself.

Curse me then. Curse Creon. No mortal will be punished more horribly than you.

OEDIPUS: Must I endure his insolence? Damnation fall upon you! Get out of my sight!
Never set foot in my house again!!

TEIRESIAS: I would never have come if you had not ordered it.

OEDIPUS: I did not know you would play the fool.
Otherwise you would have waited a long time to be called.

TEIRESIAS: The fool? Ha! Your parents thought me wise enough.

OEDIPUS: My parents? Who were they? Speak.

TEIRESIAS: This day will give you a father and lead you to your grave.

OEDIPUS: You know only how to speak in the darkness of riddles.

TEIRESIAS: I thought you were the man who could unlock a riddle's secret.

OEDIPUS: Yes! Mock me for the skill that made me great.

TEIRESIAS: A greatness that will be your ruin.

OEDIPUS: I saved this city!

TEIRESIAS: It is time to leave. Come, boy.

OEDIPUS: Yes, take him away. Leave me in peace.
Your presence here disturbs my world.

TEIRESIAS: I go. But first I will tell you why I came. I am not afraid of you.
You cannot do me harm.

Hear me: the man you seek with your edicts warrants and decrees—the man who killed the king—that man is here.

You think of him as foreign-born. But he is a Theban.

His good fortune will turn to sorrow. Though he has eyes, he will be blind.

Though he wear purple, he will wear beggar's rags.

Leaning upon his staff, he will tap the earth that leads him into exile.

To his children he will be both brother and father.

To her who gave him birth both son and husband.

And to his father he will be both killer and the man who shared his bed.

Go in now and think upon my words.

If you find that I have not spoken truth, then you can say I have no gift for prophecy.

(exit Oedipus, Teiresias, and boy)

CHORUS: The Oracle at Delphi has spoken.
But who is the man who took the blood of kings?
Who is this man of unspeakable darkness?
He must fly like the wind's swift steeds.
For on his heels Apollo races
In the blinding light of his father's fire.
And ever on his track the Furies follow hard
Like hounds scenting blood.

Holy Parnassus! Blinding peak of snow!
You flash to earth the icy will of the gods.
Find the killer. Find the man who roams
Like a bull in the forest's shadow,
Raging in the haunting dark as his doom hovers,
Ready to strike.
There is nowhere to hide from the light
Of Apollo's shrine,
When voices divine hunt him down.

The man skilled in the beating of the wings of birds
Troubles me deeply. Is there truth in his art?
I am lost. I have no words. I can see neither
Past nor future. I am adrift on the wind.
There was no quarrel ever that I knew
Between our royal house and Polybus, father of
our king.
There is no proof. How then can I question his
honor
And in a feud of blood pursue this untracked mur-
der?
Zeus and Apollo know all things,
Know the ways of mortal men.
But that a prophet knows more than I,
What proof is there? One man may possess
More wisdom than another. So how can I—
Without the truth before my eyes—cast blame
Upon my king?
He saved our city from the Sphinx
Was tested hard and shone like gold.
To my mind he is wise and guilt-free.

(enter Creon)

CREON: My fellow citizens, I have come here to lodge
a protest.
I have heard that Oedipus has accused me of a
grievous charge.
If he thinks that I have harmed him—by my ac-
tions or in words—in this present crisis then I
put no value on my life in face of this dishonor.
For I am not being accused of some minor private mistake.
I am charged with being a traitor to the state and to
you, my friends.

CHORUS: The king was angry. His words were rash. He
was not thinking when he spoke.

CREON: Did anyone dare to suggest that I had urged the seer to bring false charges?

CHORUS: Such things were mentioned. I do not know why.

CREON: How did he look? Surely he must have been out of his senses when he made this hideous accusation?

CHORUS: I do not know. It is not for me to judge the behavior of my king.

(enter Oedipus)

OEDIPUS: You there! What are you doing here?
Do you have the gall to come near my palace?
There is no doubt in my mind that you planned to kill me and usurp the throne.
Tell me, did you think I was a fool or a coward?
Is that why you hatched this plot against me?
Did you think I was too stupid to see your slithering treachery—too frightened not to fight back?
You are the fool if you think you can get the crown without the support of friends.
A crown must be fought for or bought.

CREON: Now you listen to me. You have spoken. It is your turn to hear me.

OEDIPUS: Oh yes, you have a silver tongue.
But how can I learn anything from my deadliest enemy?

CREON: First, I would prove that those words are not true.

OEDIPUS: That you are not my enemy?

CREON: You are headstrong and stubborn. Change your ways.

OEDIPUS: And you are a fool if you think a man can betray his family and get away with it.

CREON: That is a fair statement. But what betrayal are you talking about?

OEDIPUS: Did you or did you not advise me to summon Teiresias?

CREON: I did. I would do it again.

OEDIPUS: How long has it been since Laius . . .

CREON: Laius . . . ? What are you talking about?

OEDIPUS: . . . since Laius left this earth in bloody violence?

CREON: I don't know. . . . It was many years ago.

OEDIPUS: Was Teiresias the city's prophet at the time?

CREON: Yes. Skilled then as now, and deserving his reputation.

OEDIPUS: Did he speak of me then in any way?

CREON: Not to my knowledge. No.

OEDIPUS: Was there no search, no formal inquiry?

CREON: Of course. But nothing was discovered.

OEDIPUS: Why did our prophet not tell his story then?

CREON: I do not know. And since I don't, I will hold my tongue.

OEDIPUS: There is one thing you know and could speak of.

CREON: What is that? I will tell you everything.

OEDIPUS: That it was *you* who made Teiresias accuse me of Laius's death.

CREON: If he accused you, you are the only one who knows of it.

But let me question you now.

OEDIPUS: Proceed. Prove me a killer if you can.

CREON: You married my sister. Is that correct?

OEDIPUS: Why would I deny it?

CREON: And as your wife and queen, she shares the throne?

OEDIPUS: She has all her heart's desires.

CREON: And with the two of you I have a third share of power?

OEDIPUS: Yes. And it is that which makes you a traitor.

CREON: Not true. Now begin to reason logically as I have. Would any man choose the troubles, the anxiety of power if he had that power but without the responsibility? I certainly would not. I have no longing for the *name* of king. I prefer to *live* like one.

Any sensible man would feel the same way. All my needs, all that I want, *you* provide.

I have nothing to fear.

But if I were king I would have to do things which I did not want.

So why should I seek the crown rather than the pleasant, untroubled life I now lead?

I am not mad. I need no greater honors than I have now.

I am welcome everywhere ... people greet me everywhere.

Those who want a favor from you are kind to me.

I know how to get what they ask of me.

So should I exchange this comfortable life for one like yours?

That would be insane. And I am not mad.
Nor was I ever tempted by the thought or shared in
  any intrigue.
If you doubt me, go to Delphi, learn if what I have
  said is true.
The god will speak the truth.
If you find that I conspired with Teiresias, then
  condemn me to death.
I will join with you in my own condemnation.
But do not find me guilty on mere suspicion, with-
  out appeal.
You cannot on a whim judge a good man bad, a
  bad man good.
A man should offer up his precious life rather than
  betray a friend.
In time you will know the truth. Time alone un-
  locks the secrets of true justice.
A wicked man is discovered in the passing light of a
  single day.

CHORUS: His words are carefully chosen. This demands discretion.
There should be no rush to judgment.

OEDIPUS: But he . . . did he not rush into his schemes,
  his plots?
  I must be as quick to counter him. If I do nothing,
  he will overthrow me.

CREON: So what is your intent . . . to send me into
  exile?

OEDIPUS: Exile? *No!* I want you dead.
  I want the world to see the punishment that trea-
  son brings.

CREON: You still resist the truth? You will not believe
  me?

OEDIPUS: Why should I?

CREON: Then you are a fool.

OEDIPUS: For protecting myself?

CREON: In the name of justice, believe me!

OEDIPUS: You are a wicked, evil man.

CREON: What if you are wrong?

OEDIPUS: I must still be king.

CREON: Even if you are wrong?

OEDIPUS: Oh my city, my city.

CREON: It is my city too!

CHORUS: My lords, keep your peace. I see the queen.
    Jocasta is coming from her chambers. It is time, oh
        it is time.
    For she alone can resolve this quarrel.

    (enter Jocasta)

JOCASTA: You are fools! Why do you shout in anger
    like this?
    Do you have no shame? The city is dying, and here
        you fight like petulant children.
    (to Oedipus) Come into the house.
    And you, Creon . . . go now.
    No more of this quarreling over nothing!

CREON: Over nothing? You are wrong, my sister.
    Your husband will send me into exile or to my
        death.

OEDIPUS: That is what I will do. For I have caught him,
    caught him plotting against my life.

CREON: *No!* Let me die amongst the damned if ever I
    wished you harm!

JOCASTA: Oh believe him, Oedipus!

31

In the name of the gods, believe him when he swears.
For my sake and for these our citizens.

CHORUS: Listen to her, my lord. I beg you listen to her.

OEDIPUS: What do you want me to do?

CHORUS: Trust Creon. He has never spoken like a fool.
And now he has sworn before the gods.

OEDIPUS: Do you know what you are asking of me?

CHORUS: I do.

OEDIPUS: Then speak on.

CHORUS: Creon has been your friend. He has sworn an oath.
You should not mistrust his words.
You should not seem to be blinded by malice toward him.

OEDIPUS: You understand that what you say means death or exile for me . . . ?

CHORUS: *No! No!* I swear by Apollo, may I die alone and cursed by the gods if ever I meant that!
My heart is dying, withering fast when I hear your anger, hear your hate.

OEDIPUS: Then let him go.
And let me die if that is what must be . . . or wander into exile in shame, leaving this Thebes that I love. You, you citizens, you move me to this change of heart. Not he . . . for wherever he goes he will be hated.

CREON: You make peace, but your words are full of hate.
Your anger still seethes within your heart.
It will come back, this anger, to haunt you.

32

OEDIPUS: Leave me in peace. Go now.

CREON: I go. You misjudged me—these men did not. *(exit)*

CHORUS: Lady, take your husband into the palace.

JOCASTA: Tell me first, what started this quarrel?

CHORUS: There were rumors. And lies breed anger.

JOCASTA: Were both to blame?

CHORUS: Both.

JOCASTA: What was said?

CHORUS: Ask me no more. Thebes is dying.
Let sleeping griefs lie in their beds.

OEDIPUS: That is strange advice, my friend. I know you
are thinking of me.
But why would you try to stop me from doing what
I must do?

CHORUS: My king, I will say this once more.
I would be called a fool if I abandoned you now.
You made this country great.
And when the winds lashed our city, you brought
our ship of state into safe harbor.
There is no one but you . . . no one who can save
us.

JOCASTA: I must ask you, my husband and my king,
what made you so violently angry?

OEDIPUS: I love you . . . love you more than all these
citizens. So I will tell you.
Your brother Creon conspired against me.

JOCASTA: Why? Why? What was the cause?

OEDIPUS: He accuses me of murdering Laius.

JOCASTA: Does he know this or is it some rumor?

OEDIPUS: He is too clever to accuse himself.

He speaks through the mouth of a prophet . . . one that he has bought.

JOCASTA: Then let your conscience rest. Hear me. I have no belief in the prophetic art.

I know. I *know.*

Let me tell you. Once long ago word came to Laius from the Oracle at Delphi—I will not say it was from the god himself . . . probably from his priests.

The word was that Laius would die at the hand of his own son . . . my child and his.

Laius . . . at least this was the story . . . was killed by highwaymen in broad daylight.

He was killed where three roads meet.

We had a son, but when he was only three days old Laius pierced his ankles, left him on a hill to die. He gave the child to others, of course, to do this. We knew then that Apollo had changed the course of fate.

The son would never kill his father.

The terror of the prophecy would die there on the hills.

That is what the prophet said, my king.

Pay it no mind. God alone shows us the truth.

OEDIPUS: A shadow crossed my mind as you spoke. And the shadow chilled my mind.

JOCASTA: What was it that touched you?

OEDIPUS: You said that Laius was killed where three roads meet.

JOCASTA: That was what we were told at the time.

OEDIPUS: Where?

JOCASTA: Phocis . . . that is the name of the town. . . .

34

It is where the road to Thebes divides, and you can go to Delphi or Daulia.

OEDIPUS: When?

JOCASTA: We heard about it just before you came. Just before you won this kingdom.

OEDIPUS: Oh what a net of death have the gods been weaving for me!

JOCASTA: Oedipus, why are you so troubled?

OEDIPUS: Do not ask me. Not yet. Tell me about Laius—how old was he?

JOCASTA: He was tall. His hair was becoming gray. He was about your height.

OEDIPUS: I feel that my own curse now begins to descend on me.

JOCASTA: I am afraid. When I look on you I am afraid.

OEDIPUS: Perhaps the seer who has no eyes can see the truth.
But tell me, tell me all you know.

JOCASTA: I will tell you everything. But now fear grips my soul.

OEDIPUS: Was the king accompanied by many men— as befitting his office or . . . ?

JOCASTA: There were just five men. One was a messenger. There was a single chariot.
He was driving.

OEDIPUS: Aaagh, that is enough, enough.
Who told you what happened?

JOCASTA: A servant. He was the only one to escape.

OEDIPUS: Is he still one of ours?

JOCASTA: No. When he came back here and found that you were now our king . . . he came to me. He touched my hand . . . he begged me to send him to the countryside where the shepherds tend their flocks. Far from here, he said. I granted him his wish. He was a slave, but he had earned this simple gift.

OEDIPUS: Can you get him back here quickly?

JOCASTA: Of course. But why?

OEDIPUS: I have been too much alone. I have asked too few questions. I need to talk to him.

JOCASTA: Then he will be here. But you must talk to me too . . . tell me of your fears.

OEDIPUS: I owe you that—oh I owe you that. For I have climbed a mountain of fear.
And I need to talk to someone. I need to talk to you.
Polybus of Corinth is my father. My mother is Merope. I grew up in Corinth.
I was a prince.
One day a strange thing happened . . . it affected me deeply . . . perhaps it should not.
There was a feast.
A man got drunk and shouted to the world that I was not my father's son.
I kept quiet that night . . . though it hurt. And I was angry.
The next day I went to see my father and my mother. I asked them about this.
They too were very angry. They said it was the mindless ranting of a drunken fool.
I found peace in that. But the suspicion lay there. Always. In my mind.

36

I knew that people talked. I could not be still. I had
to leave.

I said nothing to my parents. I went straight to Delphi, to the oracle. I questioned him.

The god was silent. He answered not a word. But
then he spoke.

He spoke of other things.

His words were sometimes as clear as the burning
sun, full of terror, pain, and things unbearable.

He said that I would bed my own mother, that I
would breed children from that womb, and that
the world would turn away in horror.

He said that I would kill my own father.

I listened. And I fled.

From that day Corinth was but a distant land
touched by the Western stars.

I moved onward, ever onward.

I never wanted to set eyes upon the horror spoken
by the god.

And I came here . . . here where Laius was killed.

I will tell you all that happened.

There were three roads that met where I was trav-
eling. A herald came toward me.

There was a chariot, horses, and a man who looked
like the man you described.

He was seated there within it.

The groom—who was leading the horses by the
reins—forced me off the road.

The man in the chariot ordered him to do so.

As the man lurched toward me I struck him. I was
angry.

The old man saw this and hit me hard with his
scepter.

I hit him back! Oh I hit him back! I knocked him
out of the chariot.

He rolled on the ground. I beat him to death. I
   killed them all! Now if that man . . . if Laius were
   part of my family . . . where then can I hide . . .
   escape from my misery? The gods must hate me.
   No citizen here must shelter me. No man must
   speak to me. I am anathema.
I have cursed my pitiful self.
Oh think, oh think . . . I have touched you with
   these hands . . . these hands that killed your husband!
I am polluted. I am the embodiment of evil.
So I must run . . . run from this city of Thebes.
But I can never go home to the land that I love . . .
   never see Corinth again.
I live in terror of killing my father and lying with
   my mother.
Ah, this was my destiny when I was born. The gods
   are cruel, savage in their anger.
You gods, pity me. You are all powerful. But let me
   never see that day. Oh let me vanish without
   trace from this earth rather than know the fate
   that makes me loathed amongst mankind.

CHORUS: We feel your anguish, my lord.
   But until you have questioned the survivor, keep
   your hopes alive.

OEDIPUS: My hopes are dying, but they will await the
   coming of this shepherd.

JOCASTA: What do you expect from him when he
   comes?

OEDIPUS: Only this: if his account matches yours, I am
   cleared.

JOCASTA: What was it I said that you find important?

OEDIPUS: You used the word "highwaymen." He said
   that highwaymen had killed the king.

If he still speaks of several killers, then I was not the
murderer. I was alone.
There was no one else. But if he says there was only
one, my guilt is inescapable.

JOCASTA: Then take heart. For this is indeed what he
said. He cannot change his tune now.
I heard it from his mouth as did the rest of Thebes.
But even if his story were to change, he cannot
make the death of Laius conform with the oracle.
Apollo said explicitly that Laius would die at the
hands of my son.
But he, poor child, never shed any blood. He died
too soon.
No, from now on I will give not a second's thought
to the words of the oracles.

OEDIPUS: You may indeed be right. But send for the
shepherd right away.

JOCASTA: It is as good as done. Let us go in. I wish only
to please you.

(exit Oedipus and Jocasta)

CHORUS: Let me walk humble in the paths of righ-
teousness.
Let my life be simple and full of awe for things di-
vine.
Let my tongue be free of arrogance.
Let me never seek too much.
For the gods live high in their imperial grace.
We alone are frail and mortal.
They live forever. Oblivion will not cloud
Their everlasting power.
A tyrant is born from a womb of arrogance.
And insolence grows fat,
Fed by empty riches.
He scales the dizzying cliffs and grasps the crown.

39

→ oedipus

But then his foot falters, falters,
And he will fall, fall and lie crumpled in the dust.
May the gods protect the man
Who loves his country,
Burns with the flame
Of his love for the state.

God is my eternal hope.
In god I trust. In god I wait for death.

But the proud man,
The man who spits in the face of justice,
The man who scorns the altars of the gods,
That man will lose his empty dreams in the whirl-
    wind of god's fire.
Greed will cut him down.
For he will never freely touch the divine
With hands that are sullied with money.
God's lightning will strike,
Strike the arrogant, strike the sinner.
In cities where there is no chorus
That will sing god's truth,
Fools will ever honor the wicked.

No more will I seek the mystery
Buried in the earth's deep core.
No more will I respect Delphi, Elis, or Olympus
If god's truth is not fulfilled on earth.

O Zeus, reveal your power!
O king, O lord of all, if that be true,
Reveal your eternal power to us!
The prophecies of Laius wither
And they die. Apollo is forsaken.
Faith and reverence are no more.

(enter Jocasta)

(handwritten margin notes: "chorus' name"; "only athenians name chorus'"; "chorus labels role as the truth tellers")

JOCASTA: My lords of Thebes, I have come here with wreaths and incense to visit the shrines of the gods.

Oedipus is deeply troubled, haunted by images of terror.

He will not trust his reason as before. The new prophecies frighten him as did the old.

He listens to anyone who speaks of disaster for our house. Nothing I say will comfort him, and so I turn to you, Lord Apollo, since you are closest to our grief.

I bring my prayers and petitions to you. Grant us deliverance from this curse.

We are like sailors in a storm when they see their helmsman's terror.

Oh help us, lord!

(enter Messenger)

MESSENGER: Friends, can you direct me to the palace of the king, or better yet to the king himself?

CHORUS: This is his palace. The king is inside. This is his wife, the mother of his children.

MESSENGER: May the gods bless her and all her house and bring happiness to everyone.

JOCASTA: Greetings to you! Your kind words deserve a kind reply. Why have you come? What is your news?

MESSENGER: It is good both for the king and the royal house.

JOCASTA: Then speak. Who sent you?

MESSENGER: I come from Corinth. The words I bring may bring you joy . . . though they are not without some pain.

JOCASTA: What is it? How can there be both joy and pain?

MESSENGER: The people of Corinth have resolved to make Oedipus their king.

JOCASTA: Is not the aged Polybus still king?

MESSENGER: No, my lady, he is dead and in his grave.

JOCASTA: The father of Oedipus is dead?

MESSENGER: If I tell a lie may I die myself.

JOCASTA: Quick! Take this news to my lord.
You oracles of the gods, where are you now?
Oedipus spent his life running from his father. He was in terror that he would kill him.
And now not his son's hand but the hand of fate has cut him down.

(enter Oedipus)

OEDIPUS: My queen, Jocasta, why have you summoned me from the palace?

JOCASTA: Hear this man, and as he speaks think of what has become of the solemn prophecies!

OEDIPUS: Who is he? What is his news?

JOCASTA: He has come from Corinth, and his news is this: Your father, Polybus, is dead.

OEDIPUS: What? Let me hear it, stranger, from your mouth.

MESSENGER: It cannot be said more plainly. Polybus is dead.

OEDIPUS: Did he die by treachery or from disease?

MESSENGER: It takes so little to send an old man to his rest.

OEDIPUS: Then the poor man died of sickness.

MESSENGER: Yes. He had lived a long life.

OEDIPUS: Ha! Oh my wife, where are the oracles now?
Why believe in the screams of whirling birds?
The Delphic god had sworn that I would kill my father.
But he is dead and in his grave! And here I stand, I
never drew my sword.
Perhaps they might argue that he died of grief for
his long absent son.
But only in that sense could I have killed him. But
no . . . the oracles are dead.
Like Polybus, their words are turned to dust.

JOCASTA: Did I not say that this is how it would be?

OEDIPUS: You did. But my own fear betrayed me.

JOCASTA: Then never think on it again!

OEDIPUS: But yet . . . I am afraid of my mother's bed.

JOCASTA: You are a mere man . . . the plaything of fate.
You cannot know the future.
So why be afraid? Live your life from day to day.
Have no more cares.
Do not fear this marriage with your mother.
How many times have men lain with their mother
in their dreams!
If you have sense in that head of yours, you will not
be troubled by such thoughts.

OEDIPUS: I want to be as confident as you. But my
mother is still alive.
And so I harbor still some fear.

JOCASTA: But your father's death is filled with light.

OEDIPUS: Yes. But I am afraid of the living.

43

MESSENGER: Who is this woman that you fear?

OEDIPUS: Merope, Polybus's wife.

MESSENGER: Why should you fear her?

OEDIPUS: An oracle from the gods filled with terror.

MESSENGER: Is it a secret or may a stranger hear of it?

OEDIPUS: It is no secret.
Apollo once prophesied that I would lie with my own mother and with these hands kill my father.
That is why for all these years I have stayed away from Corinth.
I traveled far but always longed to see my parents' faces.

MESSENGER: This was the fear that turned you into an exile?

OEDIPUS: And the fear of killing my own father.

MESSENGER: Well, since I came to bring you pleasure, why should I not free you from this fear?

OEDIPUS: You would be well rewarded.

MESSENGER: I confess I hoped to profit when you returned to Corinth.

OEDIPUS: I will never go near my parents' home.

MESSENGER: Then, my son, you do not know what you are doing.

OEDIPUS: How so, old man? Tell me all you know.

MESSENGER: Is this why you are afraid to come home?

OEDIPUS: Yes. In case the word of the gods comes true.

MESSENGER: You are afraid that you will be cursed through your parents?

44

OEDIPUS: I fear it now—I have feared it always.

MESSENGER: My son, your fears are baseless.

OEDIPUS: How baseless?

MESSENGER: Polybus had no blood ties to you.

OEDIPUS: Are you saying that Polybus was not my father?

MESSENGER: No more your father than I am.

OEDIPUS: But you are nothing to me.

MESSENGER: Nor was he.

OEDIPUS: Why then did he call me his son?

MESSENGER: Long ago I gave you to him as a gift.

OEDIPUS: What! But he loved me like a son.

MESSENGER: He had no children of his own. You touched his heart.

OEDIPUS: Was I a foundling . . . did you buy me?

MESSENGER: I found you in the woods of Cithaeron.

OEDIPUS: What were you doing there?

MESSENGER: I was a shepherd. I tended the mountain flocks.

OEDIPUS: A wandering shepherd . . . a hired hand?

MESSENGER: Yes—but the man who saved your life.

OEDIPUS: Saved my life? How? From what?

MESSENGER: Your ankles will tell the story.

OEDIPUS: Why remind me of my childhood pain?

MESSENGER: I removed the pin that bolted your feet together.

OEDIPUS: Yes . . . from my earliest memory I have had that mark.

MESSENGER: That is why you were given your name.

OEDIPUS: Who did it? My father, my mother? Tell me.

MESSENGER: I do not know. The man who gave you to me may know more.

OEDIPUS: I thought it was you who had found me.

MESSENGER: No, another shepherd gave you to me.

OEDIPUS: Who was he? Can you tell me who he was?

MESSENGER: He was one of Laius's household.

OEDIPUS: The man who was once the king?

MESSENGER: Yes. He was a herdsman for King Laius.

OEDIPUS: Do you know if he is still alive?

MESSENGER: These Thebans here could better answer that.

OEDIPUS: Does any one of you know this shepherd?
Have you seen him in the fields or in the city? An-swer me right away.
It is time to clear this matter up.

CHORUS: I think he is talking about the very man that we have sent for.
But Queen Jocasta would know better than I.

OEDIPUS: Do you know this man we sent for? Is this the man the stranger speaks of?

JOCASTA: What man? Why does it matter? Leave it alone.
It is a waste of time to worry about such trivial things.

OEDIPUS: Trivial? I cannot find out the secret of my birth!!

46

JOCASTA: If you care for your life . . . stop now. No more! My pain is hard enough.

OEDIPUS: You need not worry.
Even if my mother were a slave and the daughter of slaves, my baseness cannot touch you.

JOCASTA: Oh listen to me. I am begging you. Seek no further.

OEDIPUS: I must go on. I must find the truth.

JOCASTA: I am only thinking of your own good.

OEDIPUS: This breaks my patience!

JOCASTA: May you never learn who you are!

OEDIPUS: Bring the man to me. Let her ever boast of her royal name.

JOCASTA: I pity you. Pity is the only word I know. The rest is nothing.

(exit Jocasta)

CHORUS: Oedipus, why has the queen left in such anguish? I am afraid of this silence.
There is something terrifying hanging over us.

OEDIPUS: Let it hang there. I have made up my mind.
I will find out who my parents were even if they were slaves.
Perhaps, with her woman's pride, the queen scorns my parentage.
But I cannot be dishonored. Fortune is my mother.
As the moons change, so do my fortunes.
If I am her child, why should I fear to trace my birth.
I am who I am.

CHORUS: If I am a prophet, if wisdom lives in me,
Then in all reverence I proclaim that you,

47

Mount Cithaeron—you are the nurse and mother
Of our king!
Before the next full moon we will worship you,
Cithaeron! We will dance in your honor,
Protector of our royal house.
Apollo, Lord, join in the dance!

Who gave birth to you, child?
Who of the immortals was your mother?
Pan, roaming god of the hills . . . was he your fa-
ther?
Or Apollo who haunts the woodland meadows?
Or was it Hermes of Cylene? Or Dionysus
Who lives among the mountain peaks?
Did he take you from the arms of one
Of his dancing worshipers
And smile the smile of a god?

(enter Shepherd and Servants)

OEDIPUS: You elders of Thebes, though I have never
seen him
I would guess that this is the man we have been
waiting for.
His age matches well with the messenger there.
And I recognize the men who are bringing him as
my servants.
But you perhaps have seen him before and know
him. I yield to you.

CHORUS: I recognize him. He is one of Laius's servants . . . a simple herdsman but honest.

OEDIPUS: Let me ask you . . . you from Corinth . . . is
this the man you meant?

MESSENGER: It is.

OEDIPUS: Now . . . old man . . . look into my eyes and
answer me all that I ask.

Were you once a servant here?

SHEPHERD: I was. A slave . . . not bought but born on the estate.

OEDIPUS: What was your occupation . . . your livelihood?

SHEPHERD: For the best part of my life I tended sheep.

OEDIPUS: What pastures did you use the most?

SHEPHERD: Cithaeron and the neighboring hills.

OEDIPUS: There you must have known this man.

SHEPHERD: Why would I . . . Which man??

OEDIPUS: This man here . . . since you met him years ago.

SHEPHERD: Offhand I . . . I can't remember.

MESSENGER: My king, I'm not surprised . . . but I will awaken his memory.
I'm sure he remembers when we both herded our flocks on Cithaeron.
He had two flocks, I one. Three long summers we were friends.
Then when winter came I drove my flock home, and he drove his to Laius's folds.
Isn't that what happened?

SHEPHERD: It was a long time ago, but that is all true.

MESSENGER: Then do you remember giving me a child to bring up as my own?

SHEPHERD: Why do you ask me this question?

MESSENGER: Because this man who stands before you was that child.

SHEPHERD: Damnation take you! Hold your tongue!

OEDIPUS: Old man! Do not curse him.
What *you* said deserved our displeasure far more than he.

SHEPHERD: Oh my king . . . what did I say that was wrong?

OEDIPUS: You refused to answer about the child.

SHEPHERD: He made no sense!!! He talks like a fool.

OEDIPUS: If you won't do it voluntarily, I'll *make* you talk.

SHEPHERD: I beg you . . . do not treat an old man like this.

OEDIPUS: Arrest this man. Seize him and put him in irons.

SHEPHERD: Alas . . . what have I done? What is it you want to know?

OEDIPUS: Did you give this man the child?

SHEPHERD: I did. And I wish I had died that very day.

OEDIPUS: And die you will unless you tell the truth.

SHEPHERD: If I tell the truth, I lose twice over.

OEDIPUS: This wicked man is still being evasive.

SHEPHERD: *No!* I have confessed I gave him the child a long time ago.

OEDIPUS: Whose child was it? Was it yours, or was it given to you?

SHEPHERD: Not mine . . . it was given to me.

OEDIPUS: Which of our citizens gave it, and from what family?

SHEPHERD: Oh for god's sake, master, ask no more!

OEDIPUS: If I have to question you again . . . you are finished.

SHEPHERD: Well then . . . it was a child of the house of Laius.

OEDIPUS: Was he born of a slave or one of Laius's own children?

SHEPHERD: *Ahhh,* I stand upon the razor's edge. What must I say?

OEDIPUS: What must I hear? . . . But hear I must.

SHEPHERD: Know that the . . . the child . . . so people said . . . was his.
But the lady in the palace, your wife, she could tell you best.

OEDIPUS: What? She . . . she gave it to you?

SHEPHERD: My king, she did.

OEDIPUS: For what reason?

SHEPHERD: To put it to death.

OEDIPUS: The child's own mother?

SHEPHERD: She was afraid of a terrible prophecy.

OEDIPUS: What prophecy?

SHEPHERD: It was said that he would kill his father.

OEDIPUS: Did you then give it to this old man?

SHEPHERD: I felt such pity for the child. I thought he'd take it to the safety of the country.
But he saved it for the worst of griefs.
For if you are indeed who this man says . . . god have mercy on you.
You were born into a life of misery.

OEDIPUS: Aaah, all has come to pass. All is true!

Light of the sun, let me never look on you again. I
  stand here, the most cursed of men.
Cursed in my birth. Cursed in an incestuous marriage.
Cursed in the murder of my father.

(exit Oedipus)

CHORUS: Oh you generations of men,
  Your life is as nothing.
  A man is bathed in Fortune's light
  And then he fades, fades, and fades into the dark.
  Your fate I pity, Oedipus, your sad fall,
  Your birth, your very birth into this world.

  Oh Zeus! His was the greatest mind of all.
  He defeated the riddling sharp-clawed Sphinx
  And won glory, happiness, and power.
  He saved us, was our tower and strength.
  We made him our lord, our King of Thebes.

  Now who is more abased, more lost than he?
  Whose life more desolate, whose grief more deep?
  Oh Oedipus! In the same safe bed
  You were both son and father!
  How could the palace walls have so long kept their
    silence?

  Time, that sees all things, has found you Oedipus,
  Condemned the incest and the guilt.
  Oh son of Laius! I wish that I had never
  Looked on you. On you I pour my grief
  As on the dead. From you I found new life.
  In you I close my eyes in grief.

(enter Second Messenger)

SECOND MESSENGER: Oh you mighty lords of Thebes!
  Oh! What you must now hear, now see!

Oh! How you will mourn if still you respect this house of Labdacus.

No river could wash the bloodstains from this house. What now lies dark will soon be brought to light—anguish inflicted—all with full intent! Self-inflicted wounds cut deepest of all.

CHORUS: Our past pains were deep enough. What more can you bring?

SECOND MESSENGER: My story is quickly told and quickly heard. Our queen Jocasta is dead.

CHORUS: Alas! Poor lady, how did she die?

SECOND MESSENGER: By her own hand. I was not there to see the horror taking place.

But I will tell you, as best I can, of the wretched lady's suffering.

She ran into the forecourt of the palace. She was in a frenzy.

Then she raced toward her bridal chamber. She was tearing her hair with both hands.

Once she was in the room, she slammed the huge doors shut.

Laius! Oh Laius! she cried, called on her husband dead so long ago. She cast her mind upon the child that he had fathered . . . the child that had cut him down . . . the child who lay with his own mother and fathered the most monstrous brood. She cursed the bed that had fathered a husband by a husband and children by a child.

What happened after that I cannot tell. For Oedipus burst in on us screaming loud.

All of us fixed our gaze upon him as he ran about in all directions.

We did not witness the last agony of her life.

For he ran up to us and demanded a sword, called on the wife that was no wife . . . the mother of his children and of his cursed self.

Some god must have entered him then in his madness.

It surely was no mortal . . . not one of us . . .

With a terrifying scream . . . as though someone called him from the other side . . . he hurled himself against the doors of her chamber.

The hinges buckled, snapped—and he rushed inside. That's when we saw her.

She was hanging there with a noose around her neck.

When he saw her he roared like a madman and unhooked the noose.

Her poor body lay there on the ground and then, oh then . . . oh the terror . . . he tore the brooches from her robe, raised them up and plunged them into the sockets of his eyes.

He shouted aloud, "No longer shall these eyes see such agony as this!

No longer see the things that I have done . . . the things that I have suffered. Those whom you should never have seen will now be shrouded in darkness, nor will you know those whom you love." And as he cried these words . . . not once but many times . . . he stabbed his eyes until the blood ran down his cheeks and matted his beard. . . . Aahhh, not drop by drop but in a stream of black rain.

This is the horror that has struck them both, man and wife alike.

Till now this house was blessed with fortune. But from this day—

Grief, ruin, death, and shame . . . all ills that have a name . . . all are theirs.

CHORUS: Is there no respite from his pain?

SECOND MESSENGER: He cries aloud to unlock the doors and let all Thebes look upon him—his father's killer—his mother's . . . I cannot speak the word. He swears that he will exile himself from this land.

He will not stay to bring upon the house the curse he himself pronounced.

But his strength has left him. He has no one to guide him.

The torture that he suffers is more than any man can bear.

He will show himself to you. Even now they are opening the palace gates.

And you will see a sight that would provoke his bitterest enemy to tears.

CHORUS: Oh pitiful, pitiful!! Never have these eyes seen such a terrible sight.

Sir, what madness descended on you?

What god has cursed you with this ungodly fate . . . you who were the most blessed of men?

Oh wretched, wretched Oedipus, I cannot look upon you.

Though I yearn to question and to learn, I must turn my eyes away in horror.

(enter Oedipus)

OEDIPUS: Ahhhh. Ahhhhhh. Pity me, pity me!

Where upon this earth am I to go in my pain?

Where will my voice be carried on the wind?

Oh god, where will it end?

CHORUS: A place too terrible to tell, too dark to see.

OEDIPUS: Yes, even now the dark holds me in its grip

Inexorable, unspeakable, eternal darkness.

The pain . . . yet again the pain. I am racked with spasms, tormented by memory.

CHORUS: The past weighs heavy on the present.

OEDIPUS: My true and constant friend!
You are still beside me. You do not forget me nor spurn my blindness.
In my private dark I still know your voice.

CHORUS: You have done terrible things. But why did you put out your eyes?
What demon set you on?

OEDIPUS: It was Apollo, my friends, Apollo.
He did this to me. He buried me in this my pain.
But it was this hand, no other's, that struck my eyes.
For why should I have eyes when there is nothing that I yearn to see?

CHORUS: It is all that you say. It is true.

OEDIPUS: What could I look on to delight my heart?
What hear or touch to bring me joy?
Now take me from this place!
My friends, do not delay.
I am, of all men, the most accursed, most hated by the gods.

CHORUS: I hear the depths of your despair but wish I had never looked upon your face.

OEDIPUS: I curse the man who pulled the bolt from my feet.
He saved my life but should have left me on the hills to die.
This heavy grief would not now lie upon me and those I love.

CHORUS: I share your sad wish.

56

OEDIPUS: Then I would never have killed my father
Nor married the woman who gave me birth.
But now my name will live on as the child unholy,
The child who defiled his mother's womb.
Was ever man more doomed than Oedipus?

CHORUS: You have chosen a painful path.
It were better to be no more than live in darkness.

OEDIPUS: No! What I have done is right. You cannot
change my mind.
If I had eyes . . . how could I look upon my father
down below?
How look upon my mother? I have sinned against
them both.
To hang myself would not wash clean that sin.
You might say that the sight of children warms the
heart.
But children born as mine were born?
My heart could not feel joy to look on them . . . nor
on the walls and temple statues of great Thebes.
No! Once I was its king—now I am nothing. I have
condemned myself to this my fate.
I have put the brand of murderer upon my own
head.
How could I have looked my people in the face?
No . . . if I had known how to stop the spring of lis-
tening, I would have done so.
I would have made this body a prison bereft of
sight and sound.
Happiness lives only where sorrow cannot reach.
Cithaeron, why did you keep me safe . . . why did
you not kill me?
Then I would never have had to bare my shame
unto the world.
Polybus! Corinth! Oh my home!
For that is what I called you then . . . home of my
ancestors, home to my infant innocence.

57

Now all is turned to filth and evil.

Oh place where three roads meet, oh hidden pathway of doom! You drank my blood!

Drank the blood that these hands shed . . . my father's blood!

You were the silent witnesses to my crime. You drove me here to save the city.

Oh marriage, fatal marriage . . . you gave me birth, and having spawned you sowed the seed again and placed upon this earth for all to see the mingled blood of fathers, brothers, children, brides, wives, and mothers.

These horrors are the worst that mankind can ever know! Take me then . . . for to speak of them is living death. . . . Take me from here with all speed—I beg you by the gods. Hide me in the earth. Kill me.

Hurl me to the bottom of the sea . . . anywhere so long as you never see my face again.

Come to me. Do not fear to touch this wretched body. Please . . . do not be afraid.

I must bear the burden of my guilt alone.

(enter Creon)

CHORUS: Here is Creon. He alone can grant your wishes.

He is now sole ruler and guardian of the state.

OEDIPUS: Ahh! what words can I find to speak? Why should he trust me?

I have treated him like a bitter enemy.

CREON: I have not come here to mock you, Oedipus, nor to reproach you for what happened in the past.

(he speaks to the Chorus) You should feel nothing but shame.

If you have no sense of human decency, at least
show your respect for the Sun, the god that gives
us light and gives us life.

Do not let this man stand here when the heavens
and the earth cannot bear the sight of him.

Take him into the palace. Only his family should
see the pain.

OEDIPUS: Hear me . . . please, Creon. You are here,
and it fills my heart with hope.

You are so noble—I so low. I ask of you one
thing . . . not for me but for you.

CREON: What is it?

OEDIPUS: Send me into exile now!

Put me in some desert where I will never again
hear a human voice.

CREON: This I had already decided. But first I had to
consult the god.

OEDIPUS: The decision was made . . . death to the fa-
ther-killer, the murderer. I am he.

CREON: Yes, that is what Apollo decreed.

But now, in our sudden present grief, we should
consult him again.

OEDIPUS: How can you ask him about such a man as I?

CREON: I can. For even you would believe him now.

OEDIPUS: Yes. I am humbled now. But I ask you this
one thing:

Grace the woman who lies within with a burial that
only you can command.

You are her brother, touch her with your love.

For me. . . . Oh never let this city—this Thebes—
be cursed with my living body.

59

No! Let me live in the hills . . . on Cithaeron. For
that is where my name will ever live.

Cithaeron was to be my tomb. My father and my
mother wished to bury me there.

Now let me find my death upon her slopes. For
that is what they wished.

This much I know . . . disease will not cut me
down, nor any common accident.

I was saved from death so I might die in grief beyond all mortal knowing.

So be it. I care no longer how fate treats me.

But my children. Oh Creon . . . for my sons I have
less concern.

They are men, and they will survive.

But my daughters . . . two sweet innocents . . .
ohhhh . . .

I can see them now . . . stealing a little of my food,
sipping my wine. Laughing.

Oh look after them.

And one last request . . . let me hold them in my
arms once more.

Let me touch them and let me weep.

Oh Creon, let your noble heart break.

I have no eyes. But I have hands. Let me touch
them, let me feel what once I saw.

(enter Antigone and Ismene)

OEDIPUS: I have no words! I touch you . . . I touch you
my pretty ones.

I hear your tears. Can this be . . . can Creon have
given you to me?

CREON: I have. I know how much you loved them.

OEDIPUS: God bless you . . . may the fates shine warm
upon you for your kindness.

Not like me! Oh my children, where are you? Let
me take you in my arms.

I am your brother and your father.

Ahh, these hands that touch you now took the light from my eyes.

These hands touched the mother that was both yours and mine!

I cannot see you, but my eyes still weep. My life to come will be a path of pain.

For you there will be only grief.

At festivals, at feasts you will skulk in the shadows. You will burst into sudden tears. And when you are ready to marry—oh god, no man will woo you, no man will brook the shame. For this shame will cling forever to our house. It will never die. Their father killed his father, spewed the seed where he himself found life, and was the father of these children here. . . . That is what they will say.

So no one will marry you . . . no one . . . you will be alone forever.

Creon, I turn to you now. You must be their father.

We who gave them life are dead. They are your family. . . .

Do not let them wander forever.

They are young. Pity them. Let them live in peace as I wander on the earth.

You must be their father now.

Do not let them be orphans of the dark . . . unmarried, beggar children. Oh pity them.

They are so young. And now they have nothing. Oh touch my hand, Lord Creon.

Swear pity.

My children, my heart is breaking.

Give me your word, Creon.

Oh my children, I wanted to talk to you.

But you are so young . . . so young.

My last words . . . find a home, find happiness, and be more fortunate than I.

CREON: Weep no more . . . go inside.

OEDIPUS: I will—but the pain lies heavy.

CREON: Weep no more. Time comes. Time comes.

OEDIPUS: I go. But I have a last request.

CREON: Tell me.

OEDIPUS: Exile me, oh send me from this land!

CREON: That is what the gods will choose—not I.

OEDIPUS: But the gods loathe my very being!

CREON: Then they will grant your wish.

OEDIPUS: Take me from this place. I am ready.

CREON: Come. But you must let your children go.

OEDIPUS: Ohhhh, do not take my children from me!!!!

CREON: You have nothing now. The power that made you great was your destruction.

CHORUS: Look on this man, you citizens of Thebes. . . . Mankind look hard.
This is and was Oedipus.
The man who defeated the Sphinx . . .
The man who became our great and brilliant king,
We envied him, we loved him, we admired him.
Now he is drowned in a sea of eternal pain.
Count no man happy till he dies.
Then, free from pain and sorrow—he may lie in peace.